The American Bestiary

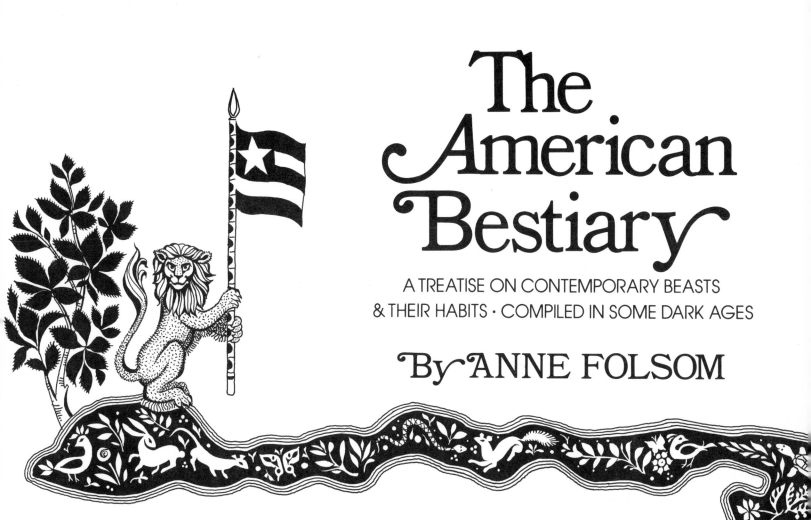

The American Bestiary

A TREATISE ON CONTEMPORARY BEASTS
& THEIR HABITS · COMPILED IN SOME DARK AGES

By ANNE FOLSOM

HARCOURT BRACE JOVANOVICH   NEW YORK AND LONDON

Library of Congress Cataloging in Publication Data

Folsom, Anne.

The American bestiary.

1. Animals—Anecdotes, facetiae, satire, etc.
I. Title.
PN6231.A5F6   741.5'973   76-20554
ISBN 0-15-105573-4

First edition

B C D E

For my parents, Hollie and Tom

without whose enthusiastic cooperation it would have been

physically impossible to produce this book

About Bestiaries

People have always been curious about animals. Even before the Middle Ages, accounts of all the animals in the universe were being collected and gathered into illustrated books called bestiaries. Some of the animals derived from the earlier mythologies of Rome and Greece and Egypt; others were observed close to home.

While bestiaries served as the first rudimentary biologies, they had another purpose as well. It was popularly held that all human behavior had its counterpart in the animal world. In pointing out the good and evil traits in beasts, the bestiaries could teach us how to lead a moral life.

Since I am a great believer in the moral life myself, I felt the time was right to launch another bestiary. Mine contains some old familiar faces, some new ones, and some that don't make any sense at all—in keeping with bestiary tradition.

I hope that by the time you have finished this book, you will have been persuaded to abandon your old ways for a pure, uplifting life.

I considered making such a change myself, but on reflection, it seemed like a pretty terrible idea.

The Tree of the Beastly Life

whose thorny branches are familiar to us all. Regular daily exercise, childproof bottles, paranoid meter maids, revised estimates, analysts on vacation—not to mention the cost of an inexpensive funeral.

The American Bestiary

The Duck-Billed Platitude

is celebrated for its ability to lay an egg. It has other talents, too: it can wiggle in a sandbox, run up a flagpole, and, if the spirit moves it, bite bullets.

It eats like a horse and sleeps like a baby. Upon arising, it tightens its belt, looking pretty as a picture. But when it gets drunk as a skunk, it is about as funny as a crutch!

The Drab Crab

works from morning till night, and what thanks does it get? It is nothing but a slave and a doormat. Up at the crack of dawn, left with the housework while all the other crabs go off to their fancy tide pools!

Just because a crab has made sacrifice after sacrifice, don't think it will receive the slightest gesture of appreciation: personal feelings don't count for anything in this world. All the drudgery will probably be over soon anyway. (The pain in its left claw is *much* worse.)

The Eff by Ibis

builds its nest on a special twig of the Investigative Branch. It can be easily recognized by its shiny black foot plumage, which does not change from season to season. Or year to year. (The first King of the Effby Ibises was very particular about appearances, and sternly commanded that all Ibises keep their head feathers short and their beaks clean—and no mating in public.)

Ibises are great hunters. They will swoop down on any creature they consider disloyal to the flock, especially those they suspect of being friendly to the Communist Partridge, such as the Ellsbird, or the Rosenbird. However, they also hunt Hijackals at airports.

In feeding habits, they differ widely from the Woodpecker, which gets its food by pecking noisily on the trunk of a tree. Ibises prefer to tap very quietly and dig for bugs on a Telephone Lion.

The Good Housekeeping Seal

frequents rather frigid places. The male seal is best known for his outgoing nature, the female for her lustrous fur and neat appearance. She works very hard to keep her self-esteem high, her habitat orderly and scrupulously clean.

Outside the home, she is extremely civic-minded. Fur ruffled, nose atwitch, she prowls for filth and stamps it out. The major objects of her crusade are the local schools of fish, where she battles courageously to remove all polluters, especially the Eldridge Beaver and the Ginsberg Howl.

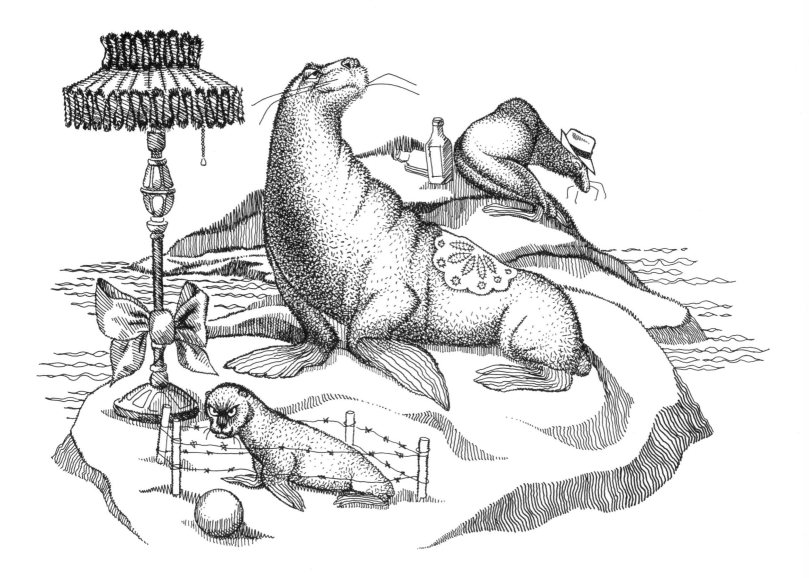

The Hippypotamus

renounces the slavery of possessions. It prefers to limit its life to the bare essentials—a small plot of grass and a quadraphonic stereo system.

Hippypotamuses like a great many things. Like, Man! Like, Wow! And Like, Maybe. They also like Old Ladies, and Dogs.

They do not like Pigs or Meadow Narks. Whenever they sense one lurking nearby, they quickly search out a supply of grass and eat all they can find. After that, they feel much better.

The Pigeon-toed Sloth

is a veritable *Guiding Light* in her unflinching *Search for Tomorrow.* Day in, day out, *As the World Turns,* she clings desperately to *The Edge of Night.*

All Her Children move in with the neighbors at a very early age.

The Lesser, or Watergate, Tapir

dates back to the distant past. It was domesticated by two species of early man: the Halde Man *(Chiefostaphopithicus),* and the Ehrlich Man *(Advisodomestipithicus).* Both had acquired the outward appearance of *Homo sapiens,* although there appears to be some question about their minds.

These men worshiped a far more powerful Tapir, the Great Expletive Tapir, believing him to be an oracle who spoke through the oval orifice. One day they were ordered to place certain secret bugs on the Donkey so that the Great Tapir might bring peace to the world. But the Lesser Tapirs were caught flat-footed in the Donkey's stable. They were sentenced to captivity for their unpardonable behavior.

Meanwhile, the Great Expletive Tapir became the Deleted Tapir. Suffering from the heat, he moved to California, where the climate is cooler; but, ironically, he himself was soon overtaken by a swarm of insects and nearly died from flea bites.

The Chocolate Moose

is eagerly sought by hunters because of its delicate flavor. It is usually served as a dessert course.

The Utterly Grossbeak

builds a ranch-style nest out of discarded Styrofoam cups. It bathes in a heart-shaped, orchid-colored birdbath. Grossbeaks are often uneasy. The young ones worry about perspiration wetness, the elderly about irregularity and beak-adhesive that won't hold properly when they peck at a Kentucky Fried Chicken.

They are very acquisitive birds, these Utterly Grossbeaks: electric feather-fluffers, nest-polishers, and worm-diggers are just some of the contrivances they manage to collect. It is the dream of every Grossbeak to own a Cattle Yak some day.

Their cultural yearnings are remarkably similar and easy to satisfy. The poems of the Rod McEwe, for example, will send whole flocks of them into a uniform coo and twitter, and Grossbeaks will migrate by the thousands to hear the song of the Wayne Newt.

They are deeply involved in the lives of their young, who are called Little Leagles.

The Male Chauvinist Pig

is sometimes called the Crashing Boar. He is a pleasant, agreeable animal which enjoys opening gates for the female, removing his hat in grain elevators, and standing up in crowded boxcars. But this above all: he never forces the sow to enter into decisions beyond her limited capacities to comprehend.

The Opec, or Wolf in Sheik's Clothing

lived affluently in the midst of hunger and poverty for many years, under what might be called a Futile System. One day, he said to himself:

"It is time to modernize. Other animals are exploiting me. I will take stock of my resources and make one or two small changes."

Getting together with a few friends, he hit upon a simple answer to the problem. From that day forward, the Opecs have taken everybody *else's* stock, resources, banks, airlines, and heaven knows what all. This adds up to a little more than small changes, as it turns out.

The Grasswapper

is usually found swinging enthusiastically on a blade of grass. Unlike the faithful Swan, who mates for life, the Grasswapper tries to preserve a lasting, meaningful relationship with its spouse by going out and having a meaningful relationship with everyone else's.

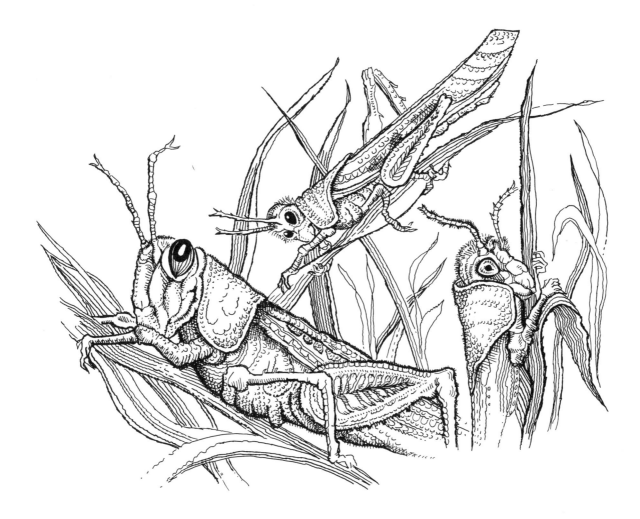

The Windshield Viper

is native to Detroit, Michigan. It is large and clumsy, with an insatiable appetite for gasoline and crankcase oil, which it must devour constantly to stay alive. Like the dragon, it belches noxious fumes—but from the opposite end.

Vipers often try to disguise themselves. Sometimes they wear fins like a fish; other times they attempt to purr and imitate a Jaguar. However, they don't fool many people nowadays because they are always big, fat, and pretentious, and they are terribly expensive to feed.

For the sake of general health, Vipers are now being bred for small size.

The Grizzly Bore

is one of a family of closely related animals including the Northern, or Polaroid Bore, and the Kodiak, or Instamatic Bore.

Bores are sensitive to light, and it is not good for them to face directly into the sun, although a lot of them do. They range over every part of the world, particularly in the summertime.

From time to time, they seek out a dark place, and hibernate for hours on end. Bores become very cross and irritable if you shine a flashlight on them when they are hibernating.

The Junk Mole

is born in a mailbox, one of an alarming number of offspring, through a reproductive process known as "littering." He is not well liked. The Mole is regarded as definitely third class because of his fawning greeting, "Dear Friend," and his incessant demands for money from total strangers. Wherever he goes, he leaves small prints, and these can cause a lot of trouble if you don't pay attention to them.

The female is even worse. She brushes mascara on her whiskers and lolls around the mailbox making lewd proposals, with nothing on but a plain brown wrapper.

The D. A. Aardvark

has a very august body, with red blood, white legs, and blue hair. She lives in an imposing grove of Family Trees, where she perpetuates her species by the process of elimination and thrives on a diet of May flowers exclusively.

The call of the Aardvark, ringing out as it proudly greets another Aardvark, is The Star-Spangled Banner—all the verses.

Aardvarks tend to be somewhat deaf, and their eyesight isn't all it might be. Because of this they sometimes have trouble recognizing the forest for the Family Trees.

The New World Liberation Badger

lives underground in a secret burrow, the better to keep out the lackeys (not-too-often-seen creatures whom the Badger nevertheless despises).

The Badger holds powerful convictions—for instance, it is obsessed with the idea that the survival of the forest depends on the total annihilation of all the huge, omnivorous, multinational animals, such as the Cartelephants.

The best way to do this, according to the Badger, is to blow up their restrooms.

The Kanguru

has a divine mission in life: responsibility for the spiritual welfare of millions of animals, including large flocks of Ash Rams. This is not easy. In fact, there is considerable disagreement among certain Kangurus on the proper way to go about it.

The controversy centers on what, exactly, constitutes a rich (nonspiritual) way of life, as opposed to a rich (spiritual) way of life. Virtually the only thing two rival Kangurus can agree on is that life, whatever form it takes, ought to be an enriching experience.

A young Kanguru who shows talent is called a Ji Whiz.

The Vampire Brat

sleeps hanging upside-down by its feet. It does this to throw a scare into its mother, but she seldom pays much attention to it. At great personal sacrifice, she gave up a promising career with the Avon Ladybugs when it was born, and now stays home and sells real estate over the phone. The Brat's father is a dentist specializing in sharks and alligators, which means he doesn't get home much.

Brats are often incorrectly classified as Aunt-Eaters because they sometimes sneak up on their relatives and bite them unexpectedly to stir up a little excitement.

Most of the time, however, they are left to sit in front of the TV set. Being precocious, they quickly tire of "Captain Kangaroo," preferring adult programs such as the popular new comedy "All in The Manson Family."

The Chip Monk

is a friendly little animal, whose favorite activity is to serve potato chips to the Archbishop at picnics of a religious nature.

The Hieronymus Vache

leads a lonely life; she has only one loyal friend. All the other cows make fun of her appearance, calling her "a mere pigment of an artist's imagination." Later on, when she is internationally famous, they will fall all over themselves for a chance to be close to her, and counted as her friend.

A similar fate befell the unusual-looking young Xer-Ox. (He turned out to be a very popular bull, when he finally got to the market.)

The Winoceros, or Wino

is a robust, full-bodied animal with a highly distinctive bouquet. It can usually be found in the vicinity of a graveyard for dead Muscatelephants.

The Unintentionally Open Fly

undergoes a wonderful metamorphosis. From a drab, uninteresting, run-of-the-mill insect, he suddenly emerges as the center of rapt attention wherever he goes.

This does wonders for his self-esteem. For the first time in his life, he finds the courage to speak up in a crowd and take a positive stand on controversial issues. As his confidence grows, he even dares to try the little jokes and wry observations he has been practicing in front of the mirror for years.

This happy state of affairs can be prolonged almost indefinitely, as long as the Fly remembers to observe the famous Mountain Goat Principle.*

*Never look down.

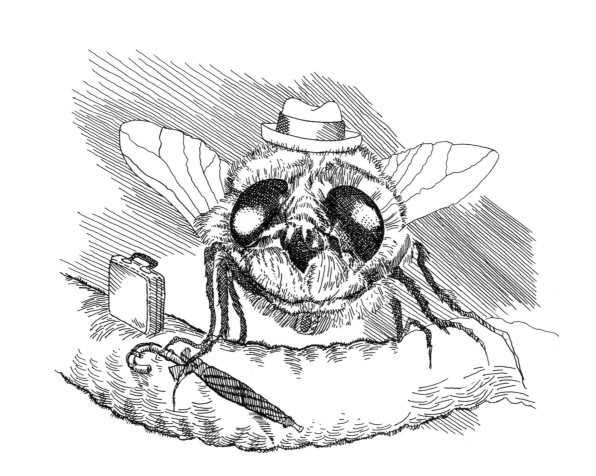

The One Can Live as Cheaply as Toucan

has a huge, ludicrous-looking bill which renders it virtually helpless against its predators, and a pouchful of plastic cards that end up causing it considerable pain. Toucans, themselves, often describe their own bills as exorbitant, and protest that it is their creditors *they* worry about.

The Toucan is preyed upon by many animals, the most remarkable being a very interesting monkey: the Primate of Interest. The Toucan is also attacked by the Wolf in Sheik's Clothing, the Soaring Index, and even religiously persecuted by the Windfall Prophet.

Without some protection, the poor Toucan will soon become as extinct as the Yak-Gnu (sometimes remembered as the Uneffete Spirochete).

The Jock Rabbit

can best be described as a fervent athletic supporter. His enthusiasm for games and sports figures goes beyond the rational. (Single-handed, he has managed to protect the Howard Gazelle from inevitable slaughter.)

The entire life of the Jock Rabbit is devoted to athletics of one sort or another. At home, he plays tennis and touch football and enters bowling tournaments. Abroad, he is equally competitive. For example, he spent years in Vietnam trying to win at the hammer-and-sickle throw. (Very similar to shot-putting. But diametrically opposite to dominoes.)

Anywhere near a frog pond, this rabbit usually goes by the name of *Jacques* Rabbit, and there is also a subspecies called the Jog Rabbit.